Also available:

The Birthday Surprise

Winter's Coming

Visitors to Stay

First published 1994 by
Campbell Books
12 Half Moon Court – London EC1A 7HE

Printed in Hong Kong

ISBN 1 85292 189 7

Fun on the Pond

Margaret Carter
Richard Fowler

CAMPBELL BOOKS

The wheelbarrow was a sad sight.

Grandma has a Ride

In their cottage in the middle of the great Ashridge wood, the Bear family – mother, father, Tim, George and Daisy – were always very happy when Grandpa and Grandma Bear came to stay.

Grandpa was very good at mending things. Every time he came he would ask, 'Is there anything you'd like me to mend, children?'

And there was always something.

This time it was the wheelbarrow. 'The wheel has fallen off,' George explained, 'and father hasn't had time to put it back again.'

'Then let's go and look at it,' said grandpa and they all went out to the shed.

The wheelbarrow was a sad sight. Lopsided.

Grandpa stood and looked at it. 'Hm,' he said. 'It needs a nail *here*, and perhaps another nail *there* . . . pass the nails, Tim and bring me the hammer, George.'

The boys ran about, very glad to be helping, while grandpa hammered the nails into place. At last the wheel was safely put back.

'That looks fine,' said grandma who had come out to watch.

'Let's see if it works now,' said Tim. 'What shall we put in it?'

'Me,' said grandma.

'You?' said grandpa, very surprised. 'You want to get in the wheelbarrow?'

'Why not?' asked grandma. 'I'll get in and you boys can give me a ride.'

She climbed in very carefully and made herself comfortable. 'Off we go!' she said.

But off they did *not* go.

However much the boys pushed they could not make the wheelbarrow move.

'You're too heavy, grandma,' puffed George.

'One more try,' said Tim . . . once more they pushed and slowly, very slowly the wheel began to turn and the barrow moved forward.

'Where do you want to go, grandma?' asked Tim. 'Just round the garden I think,' she answered. 'And be careful, boys – don't tip me into the flower beds.'

The boys laughed so much at the thought of grandma among the flowers that the wheelbarrow began to wobble from side to side.

'Steady, boys, steady,' called grandpa.

'I know where we can go,' said George, 'we can go and see if any of our tomatoes are ready to be eaten.'

A few weeks earlier the children had each planted some tomato seeds into three big pots. Father had written a name on each pot and now the plants had grown tall and strong.

Hidden among the leaves were lots of little green tomatoes, waiting to turn red when the sun shone on them. 'Oh look,' Tim cried, 'there are some red ones on Daisy's plant.' Sure enough, peeping among the green tomatoes were several bright red ones. 'Can we pick them and take them home?' George asked.

'Mm, mm, mm,' said Daisy. 'They're Daisy's tomatoes, so Daisy must carry them,' said Tim. But this was difficult as Daisy was too small to carry them all. 'Put them in my hat,' said grandma – and that's how Daisy carried them all safely home.

Mother made them into sandwiches and there was enough for one sandwich each. 'There is nothing so good,' said father, 'as a tasty home-grown tomato. Thank you, Daisy.'

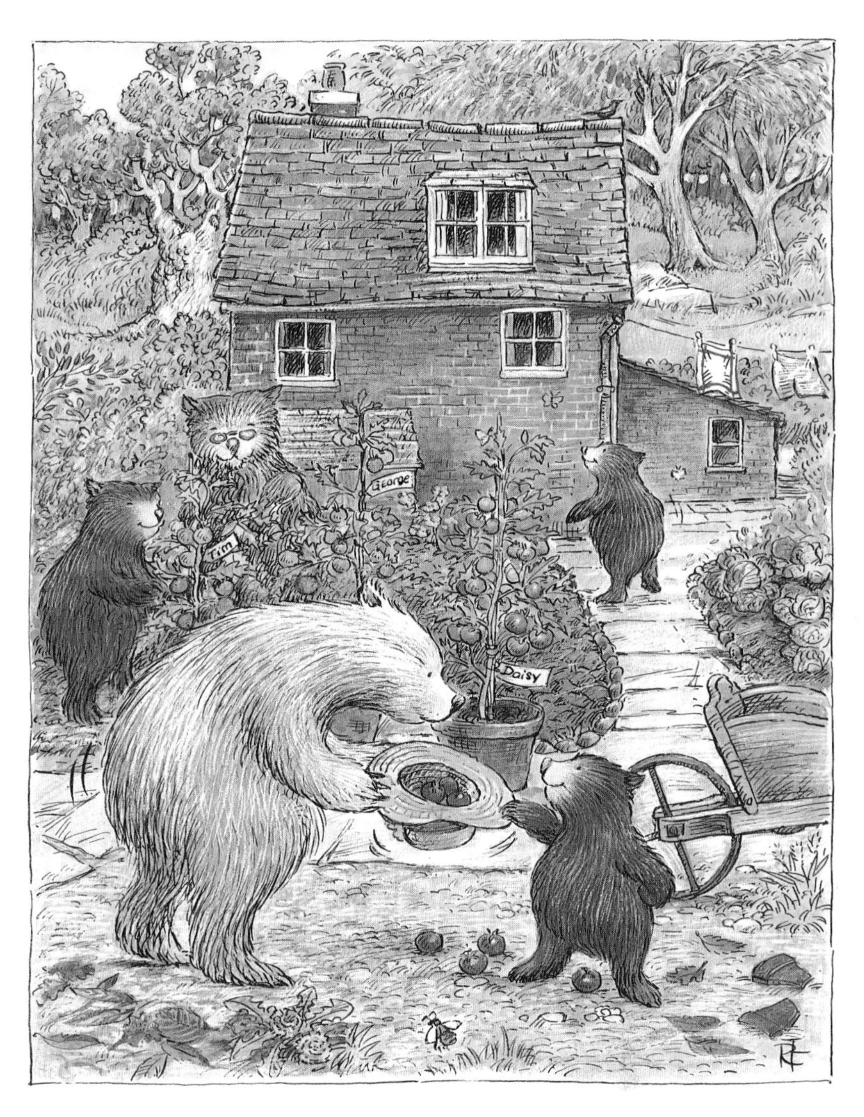

'Put them in my hat,' said grandma –

'Grandpa,' said Tim, when the last sandwich had been eaten, 'you're so good at mending things, do you think you could mend our old rocking horse? His head has fallen off and his rockers won't rock any more.'

'Well, I could try,' said grandpa, 'although I don't think it will be very easy. But I have made something else for you – something I think you'll enjoy.' 'What, grandpa, what?' the children wanted to know. 'Wait and see,' said grandpa. 'You'll know tomorrow.' And he gave a big, secret smile.

Fishing with Grandpa

The first thing Tim saw when he woke up were his green wellies. They were standing by the door and next to them were George's wellies. And inside one of each pair of boots was a fishing net. Then he remembered what grandpa had said last night. 'I've made something for you – wait until tomorrow and you'll see.'

'George, George,' he cried. 'Wake up! Look what grandpa has made for us.'

'What . . . what . . .' George was still sleepy as he tried to sit up in bed. Then he saw the fishing nets. 'Oh my!' he gasped. 'Fishing nets! Come on, Tim, let's find grandpa!'

'I wonder if grandpa made Daisy a net as well?' Tim asked as they hurried downstairs. They peeped round her bedroom door, then they began to laugh. Daisy was sitting up in her cot. She had put a boot on each paw and in her fishing net she had put one of her dolls which she was wagging about.

'Fishing nets are for fishing,' said Tim. 'Not for giving your doll a ride.'

They lifted her out of her cot and hurried downstairs to where grandpa was reading his newspaper. ‘Grandpa, grandpa, did you really make those fishing nets for us?’ they asked.

‘Fishing nets, boys? I don’t know what you mean,’ said grandpa but they knew he was laughing behind his newspaper.

‘Don’t tease us, grandpa! Will you really take us fishing?’

‘Perhaps, perhaps,’ grandpa said. ‘And me, me, me, too,’ cried Daisy, waving her net around in a dangerous way.

‘Breakfast first,’ said mother.

They were all so anxious to go fishing that they didn't eat much breakfast but at last they were ready.

'Off we go, then,' said grandpa.

'Oh do be careful of Daisy,' said mother. 'She's very small, and you must all look after her.' 'I promise,' said grandpa. 'The water isn't at all deep – it's only really like a puddle and I promise I'll hold her hand all the time.'

As soon as they reached the pond they all waded in. Grandpa kept his promise and held Daisy's hand and they all began to fish.

They caught all sorts of things: a few snails, two tadpoles, lots of weeds and twigs and some fat wet leaves. But no fish. Then at last, 'A fish! A fish!' they cried.

Daisy was holding up her net and inside, squirming and wriggling – was a very small shiny fish.

– next minute they were all sitting in the pond –

‘Oh well done, Daisy,’ said grandpa.

‘Clever old Daisy,’ said George.

They all had a very good look at the little fish (which also had a very good look at all of them). Then it was time to put it back into the pond.

‘Bye, bye, fish,’ said Daisy, turning her net upside down. The fish wriggled and jumped, then – instead of sliding back into the pond, it slipped inside Tim’s boot!

‘Oh! Oh!’ yelled Tim hopping around on one foot. ‘Take it out! Take it out! It’s tickling me!’

‘Stand still!’ called George who just could not stop laughing. ‘Stand still!’ he called again . . . but too late . . . SPLOSH! Tim had sat down in the pond. As he fell he tried to catch hold of George, who tried to catch hold of grandpa . . . next minute they were all sitting in the pond, with Daisy on grandpa’s lap.

Back at the bears' cottage, Mother and Father Bear were enjoying a quiet chat with grandma when they heard a very strange sound. *Splish, Splash, Splosh*, it sounded.

'Whatever's that?' asked father and they all went to the door to see what could be making such a noise.

And then – they all began to laugh. Mother laughed, grandma laughed, father laughed. They held their sides and they all laughed and laughed – because, outside stood three very small bears and one large bear.

All very wet. All very miserable.

'We sat down in the pond,' said grandpa.

'But I did . . . c . . . c . . . atch a fish,' said Daisy. 'You'll catch a cold as well,' said mother, trying hard to stop laughing.

'Never mind,' said grandma, 'come in and get nice and warm and I'll make you a drink to cheer you all up.'

That night, when the boys were getting ready for bed, Tim looked out of his bedroom window.

'There's a light on in the shed,' he said, 'and I can hear hammering and sawing. I think grandpa must be making something else for us.'

But George was giggling. 'You did look so funny, Tim, with that fish in your boot!'

'So did you when you sat down,' said Tim, plopping his brother on the head with a big soft pillow. 'Go to sleep, boys,' called up father. But even when they were almost asleep they could still hear the sound of sawing from the shed – and still the light was burning. . . .

Grandpa's Surprise

When the bear children came down to breakfast they were very surprised to find that grandpa was not sitting reading his newspaper as he always did every morning.

'Grandpa has gone for a walk,' explained father. 'He got up very early this morning.'

The boys were astonished. 'But he never goes for a walk without us,' they said.

'You were still asleep when he went,' said mother. 'But when you've finished your breakfast, why don't we make a picnic and go to meet him?'

'I love picnics,' said grandma. 'I could make some honey cakes to take: will you help me, children?'

The three children cheered up at once. They all liked grandma's honey cakes and they all liked helping her to make them because she let them take turns with stirring the mixture and then plopping it into the cake tins ready to be cooked.

After breakfast, mother began to cut some sandwiches while grandma put on her apron and brought from the larder all she'd need to make the cakes.

'We'll need a lot of food,' said George. 'There will be five, six . . . no *seven* of us to eat it.' 'And it will be very heavy to carry,' said father.

'I know,' said Tim, 'why don't we put it all in the hamper and then put the hamper in the wheelbarrow?' 'Good idea,' said father.

As soon as the food was ready, they packed it into the hamper – the cakes smelt delicious – and put the hamper carefully in the wheelbarrow.

'What a good thing it's mended,' said mother.

'Does grandpa know where to meet us?' Tim asked as he helped to wheel the barrow.

'Oh yes – he won't be far away. Why, look, there he is – waiting for us. I can see him through the trees.'

'Let's run,' said George. 'Chase me, Tim!'

Off he went, running as fast as he could with Tim close behind. In the distance they could see grandpa waiting for them. He was standing by the pond and although it was far away they could see the sun shining and sparkling on the blue water. 'Oh Tim, look!' George whispered and he stopped so suddenly that Tim nearly bumped into him. George pointed.

Floating on the pond was a boat – but this was no ordinary boat. It was made of wood and there was room inside for two or three small bears to sit down. But it was the front of the boat that was different. Riding proudly like one of the old pirate ships was a carved head. The eyes were round and looking straight ahead. 'Why,' said George, 'it's, it's . . .'

'It's our rocking horse,' said Tim.

'Grandpa has made our rocking horse into the front of a boat,' whispered George.

'I told you we'd find a use for him,' said grandpa, coming to meet them. 'You may not be able to ride on his back any more, but now you can sail in him instead.'

The boys were really too astonished to speak: they could only stand and stare at their wonderful boat.

'Can we really sail in her?' whispered Tim.

'Of course,' said grandpa.

Floating on the pond was a boat –

By now the others had caught up with them and were standing smiling at the children's surprise. 'I think you all knew what grandpa was making,' said George.

'Well, maybe,' laughed grandma.

Very carefully the boys climbed into the boat. 'Oh, is it safe for Daisy?' mother asked.

'Of course,' father said. 'The pond is only as deep as a puddle. Even if she fell in she'd only get a bit wet. And we're all here to watch.'

'Do look after her, boys,' said mother.

The boys each put an arm round Daisy and kept her between them. 'Don't worry, mother,' Tim said. 'We're holding her tight.'

Father gave the boat a gentle push. It wobbled, then it wobbled a bit more. They all held their breath . . . but then very slowly and quietly it floated into the middle of the pond.

'Hooray!' they all cried.

All that day they sailed and sailed. They even ate their picnic in the boat, while the grown ups watched from the shore. But at last it came to an end. 'Time to go home,' called father.

They tied the boat safely to the stump of a tree and walked home, Daisy riding on grandpa's shoulders and the boys each holding one of his paws. 'Our boat is the best thing you've ever made,' whispered George. And grandpa smiled.

That night the children dreamed about their boat, knowing it waited for them, still and safe among the rustling reeds, ready to welcome them to another day of happiness.